I GOT THIS HAT

Written by
Jol and
Kate Temple

Illustrated
by Jon Foye

ABC
Books

The ABC 'Wave' device and the 'ABC KIDS' device are
trademarks of the Australian Broadcasting Corporation and
are used under licence by HarperCollins*Publishers* Australia.

First published in Australia in 2013
Paperback edition published in 2014
by HarperCollins*Children's Books*
a division of HarperCollins*Publishers* Australia Pty Limited
ABN 36 009 913 517
harpercollins.com.au

HarperCollins*Publishers*
Level 13, 201 Elizabeth Street, Sydney NSW 2000, Australia
Unit D1, 63 Apollo Drive, Rosedale, Auckland 0632, New Zealand
A 53, Sector 57, Noida, UP, India
1 London Bridge Street, London SE1 9GF, United Kingdom
2 Bloor Street East, 20th floor, Toronto, Ontario M4W 1A8, Canada
195 Broadway, New York NY 10007, USA

National Library of Australia Cataloguing-in-Publication entry:

I got this hat / written by Jol and Kate Temple ; illustrated by Jon Foye.
ISBN: 978 0 7333 3206 7 (hbk.)
ISBN: 978 0 7333 3230 2 (pbk.)
For children.
Hats—Juvenile fiction.
Stories in rhyme.
Temple, Kate.
Foye, Jon.
Australian Broadcasting Corporation.
A821.4

Designed by Jon Foye
Colour reproduction by Graphic Print Group, Adelaide
Printed in China by RR Donnelley on 140gsm Woodfree

9 8 7 6   16 17 18 19

Hats off to Arlo & Clancy!

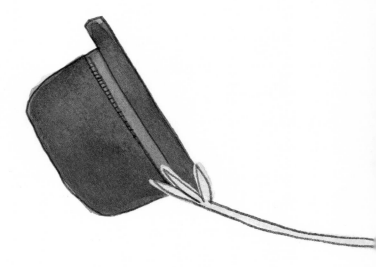

"I GOT THIS HAT IN CHINA"

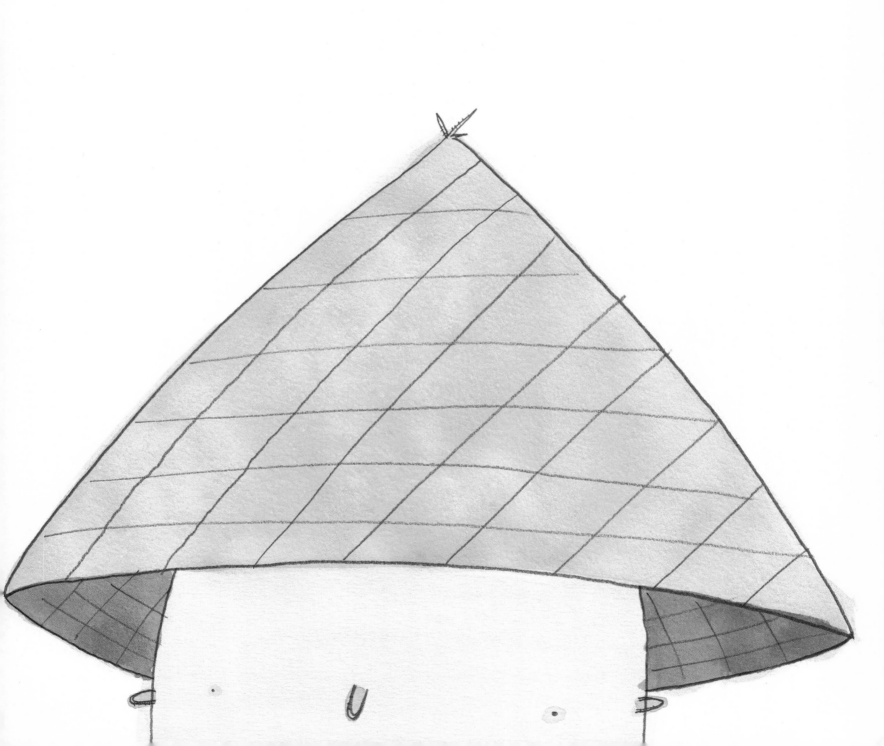

"I GOT THIS HAT from a MINER"

"I GOT THIS HAT FROM A DEEP-SEA DIVER"

"I GOT THIS HAT FROM ___a racing car___ DRIVER"

"I GOT THIS HAT from a PILOT"

"I GOT THIS HAT FROM A PIRATE"

"I GOT THIS HAT

On a tropical

ISLAND"

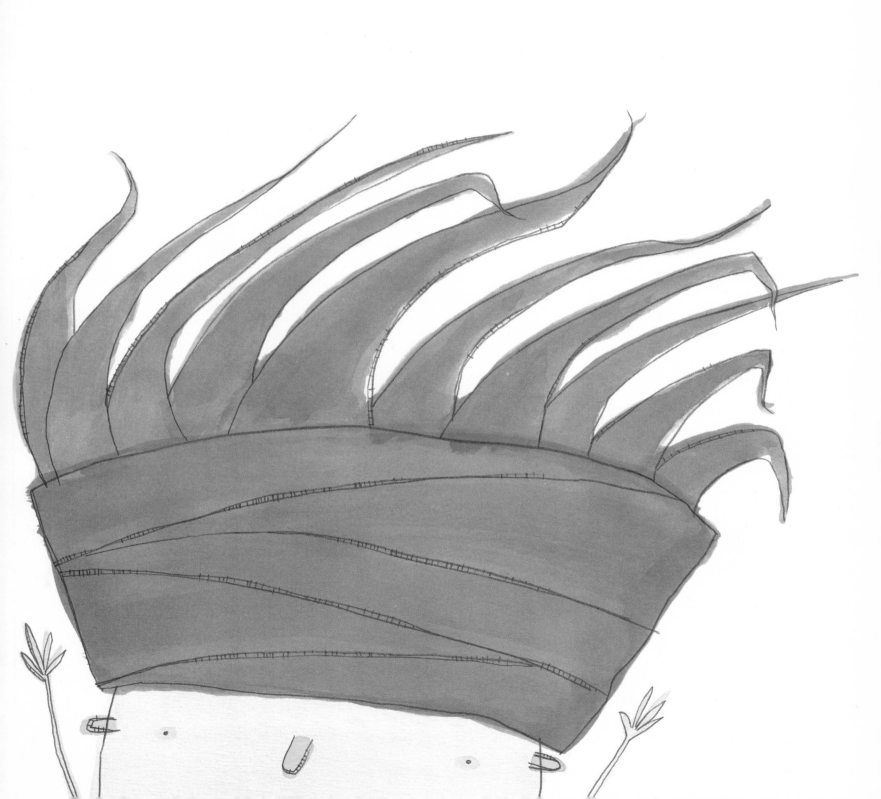

"I GOT THIS HAT from the SCOTTISH HIGHLANDS"

"I GOT THIS HAT FOR BIKING"

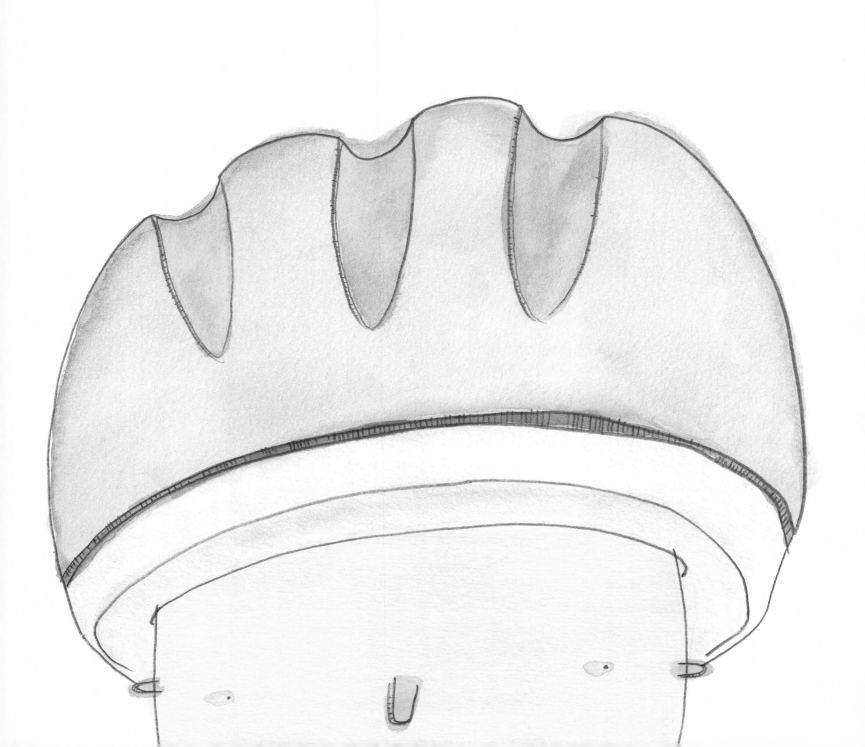

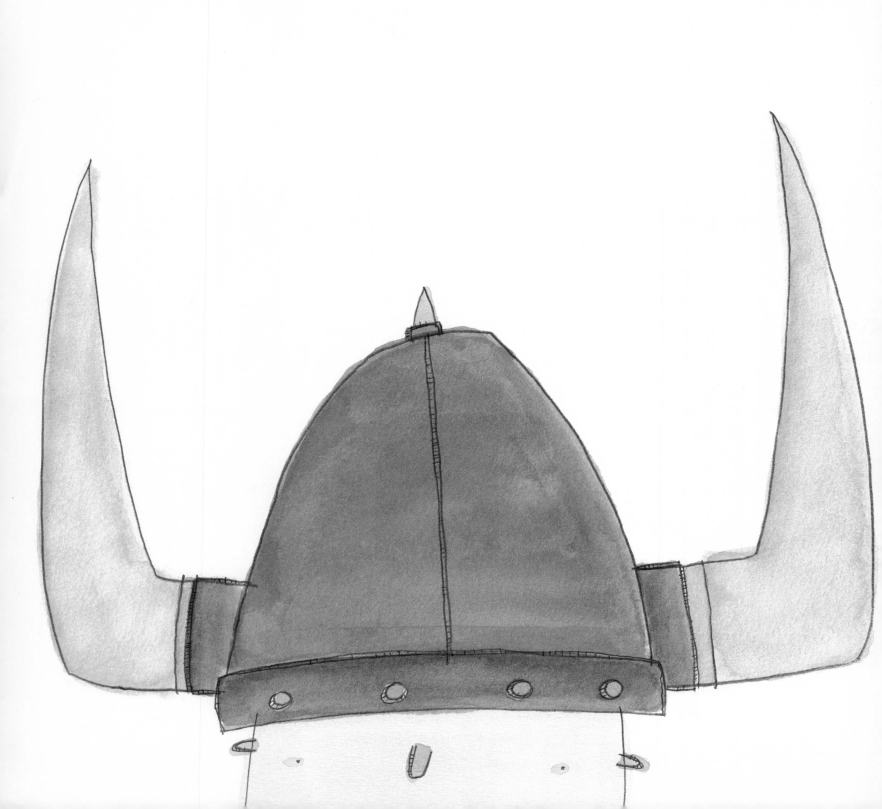

"I GOT THIS HAT _from a_ VIKING"

"I GOT THIS HAT

from an

ESKIMO"

"I GOT THIS HAT IN MEXICO"

"BUT TO BED I'll Wear

TO BED

"NONE!"

Jol & Kate Temple

Kate and Jol enjoy wearing hats together. They wear them whenever they write. Jol prefers a fedora, Kate a fez. When in San Francisco they bought a hat from an ex-girlfriend of Clint Eastwood. Kate and Jol have written five books for children and they live in Rozelle, with their hat-wearing boys Arlo and Clancy.

Jon Foye

Jon is a big fan of the raccoonskin cap. He wears one continually when illustrating books. Jon also owns a jaunty alpine hat that he wears in semi-professional yodelling contests. Jon has illustrated three books written by Kate and Jol including *Mike I Don't Like*, which was awarded Best Designed Picture Book in Australia. Jon lives in Rozelle with his wife Marissa and baby boy Archie, who has a thing for berets.